Best Wishes

Sally Cronin

TALES
FROM THE
GARDEN

by

Sally Cronin

Moyhill Publishing

Print Edition 2015
ISBN 97819055974642.

Printing History:
First published in 2015 by Moyhill Publishing.
Print Edition ISBN 97819055974642.
MOBI ISBN 978190559659.
EPUB ISBN 9781905597666.

Photo Credit: Boxer Puppy photograph courtesy of Andrea Cañón
"A two-month-old fawn Boxer puppy."
Licensed under the Creative Commons Attribution 2.0 Generic license.

The papers used in this book were produced in an
environmental friendly way from sustainable forests.

Moyhill Publishing.
Suite 471, 6 Slington House, Rankine Rd., Basingstoke, RG24 8PH, UK.

Dedication

This book is dedicated to Mollie Eileen Coleman

October 5th 1917 – July 28th 2012

The Duchess.

Acknowledgements

My thanks to Diana Hayden and Miss Ellie for allowing me to take photographs of their lovely garden used for Trouble in Paradise. Also to my mother Mollie Coleman for always making a garden for us to enjoy with colourful displays all year round.

Thanks also to Geoffrey Cronin for allowing us to photograph his lovely garden, in Ireland, for the Winter Fairy.

Always my thanks to my husband David who takes my words and vision for a book and turns it into a reality. There would be no book without him.

Contents

1. The Head Guardians of the Magic Garden............1

2. The Sanctuary..7

3. The Last Emperor 13

4. Pearly Girl and the Dwarves Stone Band............21

5. Trouble in Paradise..28

6. Little Girl Lost..45

7. The Goose and the Lost Boy...............................50

8. The Boy, his Dog and a Fairy Princess 64

9. The Last Summer Ball and the Winter Fairy.........73

10. Mollie (The Duchess) Coleman 91

About the Book 108

About the Author..109

Also by Sally Georgina Cronin............................110

    Size Matters 111
    Forget the Viagra … Pass Me a Carrot!............112
    Just Food For Health 114
    Sam, A Shaggy Dog Story...................................115
    Turning Back the Clock 116
    Media Training: The Manual 117
    Just an Odd Job Girl...118
    Flights of Fancy..119

Chapter 1
The Head Guardians of the Magic Garden

We have stood guard for fifty years over this house and the people who have lived here. Protecting the land and our masters against unwanted intrusions in scorching sunlight and bitter cold snow. The world has changed outside these walls with dictators passing on to make way for kings.

But that is not our concern, as it is the safety of this place that is our responsibility.

Through many seasons we have watched young children play in front of us with their dog companions. We have observed the young humans mature and grow to adulthood before leaving through the black gate that leads to the outside world. And we have seen their canine companions grow stiff with age and sheltered them as they rested in the shade we cast.

For the last five decades we have observed the man who trims the evergreen hedge that surrounds us. We have watched him change from a vital young man to the weather-worn 82-year-old who still sweeps his brush around our feet. If we could see our own reflections we know we would also show the effects of all these years with our faces to the sun and wind.

We have not seen him this past hot summer. His weary bones could no longer hold him erect as he carried his tools and watered the expanse of grass. He decided one spring morning that he would retire to his nearby home and enjoy his plants on his balcony. As he left through the big black gate, he turned and looked at us as we stood with unseen stone tears upon our cheeks.

He saluted and smiled in acknowledgement and to remind us that we must continue to protect the garden on his behalf.

The gnarled branches of the green plinth that sits beneath us also bears the scars of time but each year it sustains its vigour. Determined, as we are, to stand firm against the elements. It too has sheltered our canine subordinates, who it should be recognised, have bravely defended the territory with us against postmen, undisciplined squirrels and disrespectful feral felines.

We rarely feel the touch of a human hand; although the lady of the house will occasionally rest hers upon our heads in passing. It is recognition enough and we are happy that our role as guardians of this house and its people is acknowledged and appreciated.

As well as the trees, plants and wildlife in this magic garden, we are the head guardians of all the other stone inhabitants who have important roles to play. Eagles, rabbits and monkeys have found their way here over hundreds of years as well as animals who have sought sanctuary within its surrounding hedges.

We are not however the rulers of the garden. Beneath the old magnolia tree, within the roots, is the fairy kingdom of Magia, which is home to the reigning King and Queen. It is our job to ensure that this realm is protected and that enemies, who seek to destroy the peace we enjoy, are dealt with swiftly.

The humans who have occupied the houses that have stood in these grounds see only statues and an old gnarled tree that blooms once a year. What they do not know is that when they lie asleep, sprinkled with fairy dust, the garden comes alive. Fairies fly out into the scented night air, statues come to life and dance in the dappled moonlight and we the guardians patrol the borders to ensure their secrets are kept from the outside world.

But, once every 500 years, some very special people are allowed a glimpse into our world. As your guides we will now tell you the stories of the inhabitants of this magic world. Close your eyes and climb upon our backs as we travel through time and imagination.

~ ~ ~

Chapter 2
The Sanctuary

Yesterday, as I wandered amongst the stunted bushes on the side of the mountain searching for food, I felt the first stirrings in my swollen belly. I had not realised that it was so close and despite being my first, I instinctively knew that I needed to find a safe place to bring this new life into the world.

In the distance I could see the herd of goats pulling at dry and thorny bushes that dotted the arid earth. I spent my nights mingling amongst them, taking advantage of their strong scent that masked my own.

They also provided safety as they were protected by the massive guard dogs from the predators of the night. Even the wild boars who feared neither man nor beast kept their distance when they saw these deceptively gentle giants.

More dangerous were the stray dogs that patrolled this rocky hillside in search of the unwary. But they too would scuttle away into the dark, with their tails between their legs and ears laid flat against their heads, at the warning growls that issued from deep within massive chests.

I had wandered far from the herd of goats in search of nourishing shoots for myself and my unborn fawn. I knew that even if I did return that they too would be scattered across the hillside taking advantage of the daylight hours. I was too exposed here and needed to find a safe place away from prying eyes as soon as possible.

I sniffed the air. A sickly feral smell filled my delicate nostrils and I could hear the sound of a large mass moving through the bushes towards me. It was the pack of stray dogs emboldened by the lack of night-time protectors. They could smell that my time was near. Despite the increasing movements in my belly I began to run and leap over small bushes away from the vile scent.

Petrified, I could hear the baying of the hounds in ecstatic and full pursuit.

I zig-zagged across the hillside dropping lower towards the houses in the distance. I skidded to an abrupt stop as I met the edge of the open ground and a metal wire fence blocked my path.

Desperately I looked around me as I heard the pack behind me closing in. I ran along the fence which was too high for me to jump and seemed to stretch for miles in each direction. The excited barking and the sounds of the pack thrilled by the chase were getting closer by the minute and I knew that I was trapped.

Suddenly I saw a small break in the wire mesh a few feet away and on the other side were bushes and the sound of running water…. I pushed my nose through followed by my ears and shoulders. It was a tight fit and the edges of the wires cut into my tender and swollen body. Finally I was through and I moved quickly into the safety of the undergrowth risking a look behind me at the dogs as they raced into view.

It wouldn't take them long to find the cut in the fence and even though it was small they would persist and barge through and find me. There was no time to stop now despite the growing urgency to push my baby out into this dangerous world. Once through the undergrowth I found a small stream which I crossed in the hopes that the dogs would lose my scent. Up ahead was a paved road leading to a large dwelling, and despite my fear of men and guns, I knew I had no choice but to try and find sanctuary within its grounds.

A smelly and noisy man made machine entered the opening in the walls and I followed hugging the hedge to avoid being seen. I heard a grating noise behind me and turned in panic to find a large black object moving across the hole in the wall. Terrified I looked around for humans but the monster had disappeared inside a large door in the side of the building.

Except for the distant sounds of the searching dogs it was quiet.

With a final jolting pain my fawn announced its imminent arrival. Desperately I searched my surroundings for some form of shelter. I saw ahead of me two large silent and still guardians who looked like those that protected the goat flock at night. I rushed towards them and saw that the hedge beneath them contained a hollow lined with earth that was just the right size to hide within and bring my young into the world.

The sound of barking died down as the pack of dogs moved away, disgruntled at having lost its prey. I could hold on no longer and as my heart calmed and my breathing slowed my baby was born.

It has been several days and as my new guardians stand watch over my baby, I wander through the lush garden enjoying the watered and abundant green grass and the delicate shoots of the hedges.

The humans who live here have seen me but have not approached and they let me wander safely with my fawn; smiling down at me from the balcony.

For the first time in my life I am not afraid and although at night I miss my strong smelling companions, I have found a sanctuary.

As I lie here in the evening sun with my fawn by my side content and filled with milk, I believe that I might stay here forever in safety, beneath the gaze of my silent guardians.

~ ~ ~

Chapter 3
The Last Emperor

High above the garden our feathered cousins soar on the updrafts caused by the scorching summer heat on the peaks and valleys of our mountain. They search diligently for their preferred prey which is anything that dares to fly beneath them or scuttle out of the undergrowth in search of food.

Majestically they accomplish what we cannot and have never been able to. From our place guarding the main entrance into the building that now stands on this ancient site, we watch enviously with our own wings fixed in stone.

We are the last of the stone eagles that have watched over this magical place. The first were made by a slave of the Roman merchant who built his villa on this mountain over eighteen hundred years ago. He and his countrymen had swept across and settled on the now peaceful sunlit Iberian Peninsula after many centuries of war. He supplied olives, figs and grapes to his fellow Romans and delivered casks of wine to the garrison of soldiers in the camp down by the river. He was a rich man with many slaves collected and bartered during the long journey from the coast to this central part of Spain.

For two hundred years the merchant's family prospered and enjoyed the life so far from their original home. The skill of stone carving was passed down from the original slave to his sons and their grandsons as the seasons rolled through the decades. But then it all changed as the Visigoths invaded from the north and violence once more shattered the peace of the land.

The merchant's family left and retreated back towards the south and eventually began a new life far away. Slaves were left behind in the panic, but being essential to work the land, were allowed to settle on farms and in small villages. But the stonemason of that time remained in the crumbling ruins of the old villa and built a modest dwelling where he continued to work and pass on his craft.

Finally his large family scattered across the surrounding area as towns and cities lured them away from the rural life. But always one remained to learn the trade and instruct another to take his place. The very last stonemason who had no sons, crafted us before he died, and as he smoothed our stone wings and hid us within the leafy folds of the boundary hedge, he muttered final words to us.

"Wait for the last Emperor, he will come and find you."

We waited and the protective hedge grew around us. The stonemason's humble home crumbled in the heat and snow filled winters, until it too joined the grand remains of the Roman villa beneath the soil.

Finally, fifty years ago, the sound of modern machinery woke us from our sleep and we watched between the large green leaves of the hedge as a new villa emerged in front of us. We heard human voices for the first time in many years and the sound of laughter as children played in the gardens.

But still we waited.

Thirty-five years passed and the children grew and left the home leaving an elderly couple rattling around its vast empty rooms. Soon they too left and all was quiet again.

One bright morning, as we lay in our hiding place, we were startled and shocked by the sudden intrusion of a long canine nose that pushed aside our overgrown covering. We stared into a pair of eyes that sparkled gleefully upon us. From this creature's mouth came forth a high penetrating noise; enough to awaken even us stone-bound creatures. Two human hands reached around the canine and pulled him gently back by his dark purple, imperial collar. They then returned and each one of us was lifted clear of the entwining stalks and leaves and we were placed in the sunlight for the first time in over a hundred years.

I won't go into the indignity of being cleaned with brush, soap and hot water in places left untouched since our stonemason fashioned us. But finally we were pristine again and placed on our ledge to guard the house as was our duty.

We remembered what our old master had said as he had hidden us from sight. And, within a short time, we knew indeed that the last Emperor had arrived, as he came before us wearing his wreath of office and informed us of his imperial title of Moyhill Royal Flush. We and his courtiers were permitted to call him Sam, but only in private.

Our joy was beyond comprehension as the prophecy was fulfilled and we took pride and delight in guarding our new master. We remained alert over the next many years as our Emperor roamed the grounds on his daily inspection, supervised the garden workers and reigned over his house slaves.

Each night he would hold court from the front balcony of the villa listening to his canine subjects in the valley as they recounted the day's events in his domain. He would wait until they had completed their report and then respond for several minutes, encouraging them to be vigilant and valiant.

He would then wait for his house slaves to bring him ice cubes to cool his parched tongue and platters of his royal repast in the form of chicken gizzards and sweet smelling Basmati rice.

We, as his loyal cohorts were not forgotten. As he passed us each day he would delicately sniff our bodies to check our health and, if he felt we were dehydrated, he would anoint us with his regal blessing.

We treasured our role as his elite royal guard and although, to our great sadness, he has now passed from our sight, we still stand sentry over him today. It is in a place where he can continue to view his great domain and listen to his many canine minions in the valley below. The last emperor has left his mark on this place, on us and on his people and will never be forgotten.

~ ~ ~

Chapter 4

Pearly Girl and the Dwarves
Stone Band

Pearly Girl and the Dwarves is a stone band that plays at all the fairy balls, weddings and birthday celebrations. To the human inhabitants of the villa, they were also playthings for the children who have grown up over the last fifty years and were loved by many.

Unfortunately, like many of the stoned rock bands of the past, the dwarves had not always behaved well. There were a couple of incidences when one or two of the band, who will remain nameless, sniffed a little too much of the pollen of the sneezeweed that grew at the bottom of the garden. They had been banned from playing at any of the fairy events in the kingdom of Magia for the last fifteen years.

The children of the house had also grown up and left and the band found themselves huddled on the windswept ledge on the back side of the house gathering moss and covered in swallow poop as the birds used them for target practice.

Finally in the late 90s the new owners discovered them in their isolated outcrop and decided to relocate the group to the top of the garden under a large shady tree where they could resume their musical endeavours without disturbing the household or the neighbours. The fairy queen, seeing that they had returned to human favour, decided to give them another chance with a dire warning of consequences should there be further unacceptable behaviour.

Although the band was tucked away in a quiet part of the garden, the abundant wildlife that had made a home in this serene spot soon began to move out. Unfortunately the dwarves were all a bit out of practice, particularly Thrifty with his kettle drum who had gone a bit deaf and drowned out the rest of the band and was asked to stand in the corner.

Shifty was on the fiddle but the others kept their eyes on the expenses. Nifty was on the saxophone, Hefty on the base drum and cymbals and Ditzy blows his own trumpet.

Wiffy tuned up his guitar and that just left Sniffy the male vocalist of the group who insisted on being accompanied by his best friend Buck the rabbit. Buck was okay as a backup singer but Sniffy failed to realise that his BFF was in fact the cause of his allergies. I know that I said that I would not reveal the names of the culprits behind the banishment from fairyland but you can probably guess that Sniffy was not blameless!

Anyway after a few weeks the band was in fine fettle and eagerly awaited the arrival of their lead singer Pearly Girl.

The fairies were holding a birthday party and tonight was the band's first performance of the summer and the first in fifteen years. Their future as a band and their chance of staying out in the garden instead of in exile on the poop covered ledge was dependent on their performance and behaviour.

Buck, as he tended to move a lot faster than the rest of the band, went off in search of Pearly Girl.

He looked everywhere and even asked the resident hippie if he had seen her. The hippie had heard that Pearly Girl and Buck's cousin Fizzy, had been on the town the night before, and might have got themselves arrested. This was not good news and Hippie and Buck hurried over to the garden's naughty corner to see if he could find out more.

They found Fizzy almost immediately, obviously still plastered from the night before and they spent precious minutes trying to get some sense out of him. Even Hippie had a go and finally they were told that Pearly Girl was the other side of the holding area in a dreadful state.

Buck and Hippie had their work cut out for them if they were going to get Pearly Girl in shape in time for the performance. Buck got the rest of the fairy juice off her and Hippie raced around getting her clothes and make-up organised. With just minutes to go and as the audience and the photographers arrived they got their star act ready.

The stage was set, the sun shone and the band began to play their first song. *'One Day my Prince will Come'* and Pearly Girl walked through the garden to join them. As she began to sing the audience broke into rounds of applause.

The fairy queen and her court were duly impressed with the two hour performance and signed a contract with the stoned band to perform at their mid-summer ball the following week.

Happy to be off the poop laden ledge for good, the band wandered off in search of the sneezeweed and a jug or two of organic rosewater laced with some fermented bee pollen.

~ ~ ~

Chapter 5
Trouble in Paradise

In special gardens you may be lucky enough to find that fairies have set up home. Since ancient times they have preferred to build their invisible houses beneath the shade of a magnolia tree. This was the case with the Kingdom of Magia in this secret garden.

The magnolia is a tree that has seen thousands of years of history and survived the earth's changes and turmoil. The fairies know that its strength will keep them safe and that its roots, so deep under the ground, will always gather fresh water to filter into their homes.

Other creatures within the garden bring their bounty to the tree as well. Bees seek out the sweetness in the blooms that form and die so quickly. But, not before little pouches of honey are stored within the heart of the flower for the fairies to collect at night. Honey is almost as ancient as the magnolia tree itself, and despite the short harvesting season, it never spoils, so can be stored in empty nut shells for the entire year.

Within the safety of the sweeping broad leafed branches and with a plentiful supply of water and honey, the fairy colony in the garden grew and flourished. Eventually there came a time, centuries ago, when it was decided that a king and queen should be appointed. A palace was constructed within the roots of the magnolia, with linked gardens and passages with vaults of golden honey. Designed to shelter and nourish the new and precious royal family it was staffed with a select number of senior fairies, who would act as servants and counsellors.

That was long in the past and the present king and queen were now approaching middle age in fairy terms; which is about 450 years old. Their subjects adored them as they were both fair to look at and generous in temperament, but beneath the surface of this idyllic royal relationship trouble was brewing.

The king was handsome, wise and had a wonderful sense of humour. All the fairies eagerly awaited the mid-summer ball but none more so than their fun loving royal master. When the ball was officially opened on the arrival of the royal couple, with the stoned band playing up a storm, he was always first on the dance floor.

He whirled his many partners around like confetti in their gossamer dresses and sparkling shoes. Their fragile wings lifting them off the ground the faster they twirled. However, he was careful to never dance more than once with any particular lady of the court. He knew from experience that the queen, who was not an accomplished dancer, would be looking on with a watchful eye.

It was after this year's summer ball that rumours of a rift in their beloved royal couple's relationship began to circulate. Not just amongst the courtiers, but also the rest of the fairies in their homes beneath the magnolia.

The king had danced with one specific and beautiful lady-in-waiting twice during the ball. It was clear to all present at the time, that the queen had not been amused. In the weeks that followed it was also noticed that she spent more and more of the day in the palace courtyard surrounded by her beloved flowers.

Occasionally a tear had been seen to fall to the blossoms beneath her. They were bitter drops of sadness and soon the lovely petals began to shrivel and fall to the ground before their time.

Beneath his stony and sculptured handsomeness, the king was also troubled, and he could be found hanging around in his own personal garden staring into space as if wishing to be miles away from the palace walls. The fairies braced themselves for bad news.

Once a week the queen would rouse herself from her sadness and tour the rest of the garden that was her domain. She liked to check in with the guardians, eagles and her other more inanimate subjects, to assure herself that the humans were treating them with respect and kindness. She also liked to pop in on the seven dwarves that made up her royal orchestra and make sure they were practicing, and not up to mischief. She skimmed across the grass towards their home beneath the canopy of an old evergreen tree with a quick visit in mind and then a return to her lonely courtyard.

Just as she was about to alight upon a conveniently placed mushroom, she bumped right into one of the dwarves who was running towards the centre of the clearing, hand in hand with a giant rabbit. Luckily for the queen her delicate body was unharmed and of course the dwarf barely noticed the brush as light as a feather

as he was so distraught and excited.

When he realised who he had bumped into he started muttering away to himself... 'Say nothing, say nothing, off with my head, off with my head.'

The queen look a little bemused... 'If you

touch my royal personage again in that manner, I will be happy to oblige' she said rather acerbically.

The dwarf looked sheepish and with his arm firmly around his rabbit for support he tried to smile bravely.

'I am so sorry majesty,' he muttered getting redder and redder in the face. 'We have just seen something shocking and we were just running to tell my brothers about it... it wasn't anything important I promise you.'

He was having trouble in looking the queen in the eye and suddenly her magical powers locked onto his thoughts.... Oh no, it can't be true...

The wavering image in the dwarf's head began to take shape and the queen focused on the silvery figures that emerged.

Dread filled her heart, and even though she could not see their faces, she immediately recognised the figure of the man as he held another body in his firm embrace. It was the king, her one love, her husband of 400 years and the man who had now broken her heart.

The dwarf was mortified and hung his head trying to hide his thoughts from his queen who he could see was dreadfully upset. He also knew that he had been in the forbidden part of the garden and should not have seen the two lovers in the first place. But he had lost his rabbit and knew that he often entered the patch of magic ivy to eat its luscious green shoots.

The queen waved him away before he saw the tears that filled her eyes…but as he turned to go she demanded that he tell no-one of what he had seen on pain of being expelled from the orchestra.

She knew that this was probably futile and over the next few hours it was clear that the story, or a version of it, was circulating amongst the fairy community and the rest of the garden inhabitants.

Life beneath the magnolia tree was usually peaceful and undisturbed and to be honest a little monotonous. This revelation about the highest family in the land was too good to keep a secret; even for those she trusted most to do so.

Her power as ruler of this invisible kingdom was in jeopardy, and if she was to maintain her status and dignity action needed to be taken. Not just to punish the king for his actions, which under fairy law meant instant banishment to the human world, but to the woman in his embrace.

The queen knew who she was. The lady-in-waiting that the king had unwisely danced twice with at the summer ball. As a member of the court and daughter of one of the royal counsellors, this floozy knew exactly what the consequences were for flirting with a married man and particularly with the king himself.

There was only one course of action and it had to be taken quickly. The queen called her trusted advisors together in the council chamber in a clearing beneath the magnolia tree. Apart from fairies she also sent out messengers to find the wisest creature in the entire garden.

Felis silvestris catus was descended from the royal cats of ancient Egypt and had wandered into this garden in Spain many years ago. He said little but when he did speak it was always profound and the words valuable.

The palace guard had led the king to an ante-chamber where he waited head in hands to discover his fate. He had tried to speak to his queen but had been held back by her soldiers and he knew that his life here in this world was at an end.

The discussions continued through the night and into the next day. Angry voices could be heard and also desperate pleading by the father of the lady-in-waiting, who was terrified of losing his daughter for good.

Eventually the doors to the council chamber were flung opened and the king was led through to face his fate.

White faced and visibly shaking the queen pronounced the sentence that would be carried out immediately. She faced the king and made him kneel at her feet. She looked down at his bowed head and sorrowfully delivered the judgement.

'You will be banished to the human world to live in another garden far away. You will be turned to stone, in the form of a one-eyed pig. You will then live beneath a wide-limbed evergreen tree that is home to many pigeons.'

The king raised his head and stared at his wife in disbelief but she returned his look coldly.

'In addition, you will be guarded by one of my most trusted ladies of the bed chamber, who will be transformed into a black dog so that she can live in comfort in the home of the humans. She will report back to me should you decide to use your own magic powers to change your form.'

The queen smiled grimly. 'Do not imagine you will be able to put anything past the Lady Ellie as she is keen of mind as well as a rare beauty.'

The king ventured to speak and begrudgingly the queen indicated that he could stand and address the court one last time.

'I am deeply sorry for my actions, but I truly love the Lady Oleander and would beg that you do not punish her for my unseemly actions.' He looked at his wife with his hands held out towards her.

'Her punishment has been carried out and you can no longer help her.'

The harsh words drew a sharp breath from the king.

'She was found waiting for you in the secret garden beneath the clock and has been frozen in time where she will now wait for you forever.'

Many years passed and the fairy world slowly recovered from the loss of their carefree king and

moved on with their lives in the heat and cold of the changing seasons within the garden.

Eventually the queen found love again with a dashing prince who was visiting from another fairy court many miles distant. As she basked in the new love, and after discussing the matter with her handsome young husband, she came to a decision.

Far, far away in the human world the one-eyed pig sat silently beneath the pigeon filled tree, becoming increasingly more decorated with their offerings. He was watched over daily by the Lady Ellie who herself had become a little bored with her restrictive life as a guard dog.

Then one day messengers arrived from the fairy kingdom having flown for three nights and three days.

The swans had acted as protectors for the tiny robin who had been sent with a message for the Lady Ellie. Now as the misty early morning sunlight filled the garden, the red-breasted bird delivered the royal decree.

The king was to be released from his stone curse but could not return to the fairy kingdom. He would now have to live as a mortal man with a human lifespan. Since the queen was now happily in love again herself and had no wish for the king to remain alone, she would also release the Lady Oleander from her vigil beneath the clock.

The Lady Ellie cast the necessary spells and some days later a tall, good looking man was seen waiting patiently at a railway station with a suitcase at his feet. After all the years of living beneath the pigeons in the tree, it was a great relief to actually have two of them pecking away at crumbs at his feet instead.

Suddenly, he noticed a beautiful young woman with flowing blonde hair walking towards him along the platform. As he heard the sound of the steam engine travelling slowly into the station, the lovely vision stopped in front of him. She smiled and reached out a hand and he swept her into his arms and kissed her passionately.

A world away beneath the magnolia tree someone else was watching the scene. The queen opened her eyes and smiled. She could now live happily ever after. Even if it was just for a brief human lifespan, her old love would now be happy too with his Lady Oleander.

~ ~ ~

Chapter 6
Little Girl Lost

I am a long way from home and find myself in a strange place listening to a language I do not understand. The winter nights are colder than I am used to and the wind is harsh as it brings snow and ice to fill my basket and numb my bare toes. Now the searing

sun is blazing down and although I have been placed in a shady place, it is not like the green and mild garden of my home.

I was given to an old lady many years ago to stand in an alcove on a bed of lobelia that frothed around my feet with soft blue. She would look out of her window from her high backed chair and each day she would fill my basket with water for the blackbird to drink from after he had eaten his sultanas for breakfast.

As the seasons passed many people would come and go along the path beside me. I would hear them say such things as 'Isn't she sweet?' and 'Such a pretty little girl'. I felt that I was special and cared for. Each new season the blue ceramic pot in front of me would hold new flowers. Geraniums in the summer and wintering flowering pansies for the winter. I loved to watch the old lady spend her afternoon carefully placing the new blooms around the rim.

As the years passed my friend became frailer and I was moved closer to the window for her to see me, but I still kept watch over the garden and the creatures that visited. On warm days she would venture outside with her stick and touch the top of my head with her frail hand.

'How are you today my fairy princess?'

Other creatures popped into amuse us at dusk. The hedgehog who stole any sultanas left by the blackbird and the fox and her cubs. I could hear the old lady laughing as she stood by the window watching them at play.

Then one day there was no more laughter behind the window. People came and went and the garden seemed to wait with bated breath. Suddenly it went dark as I was covered by many layers of popping material and I could not see. I was packed tight

between boxes and for many days I was bounced between them.

When my eyes were uncovered I found myself alone on a balcony without friend or foxes. And I was sad. But then one morning I woke to find that with the sun, had come new friends, and in my basket were special stones from around the world that had been given to me to safeguard.

I had been placed on a step with a view over the garden and mountains and strong companions stood beside me to keep me safe.

I am happy now and whilst I miss the old lady I have my friends and a place by the front door where all that come and go can see and talk to me. My new mistress whispered to me as she placed another stone in my basket. "Wherever we go; you will go with us little fairy princess".

~ ~ ~

Chapter 7
The Goose and the Lost Boy

Ashort walk from the magic garden was a lake filled with fish and home to waterfowl of every description. The ducks had lived in peace for many years and had grown old and fat on the luscious green shoots that flourished close to the water's edge.

Occasionally a goose or two would fly in and rest their weary wings during one of their long migrations between the northern lands and Africa. One bright afternoon a pair of young feathered lovers arrived and settled in for the night amongst the bushes. The female was weak and sick and her mate stood over her as she lay exhausted in the grass.

When the morning sun sent a blush of gold across the blue of the lake, a sorrowful song was heard by the inhabitants of this water world as they awoke from their slumber.

Instead of leaving and continuing his migration, the male goose prowled the lake, honking at any fowl that crossed his path. He was wild with grief and could not leave his mate behind. This carried on for several days until he too became weak with hunger. He lifted himself out of the water to die beside his beloved.

As he laid his weary head upon the ground he heard a goose cry from the other side of the lake. A call from one of his own kind. In desperate need of comfort, he rose unsteadily and slipped back into the mountain cold water. He headed towards the sound and searched from side to side to find the one who was calling him.

Instead of a goose he saw many of the large ducks who had previously annoyed him, clustered around a large animal. He had not come across any humans before, but if he had, he would have recognised the figure as an old woman, in a tatty grey coat, sitting on some rocks just out of the water. She was making honking noises and clucking with her tongue as her entourage of ducks clustered excitedly around her.

Intrigued the goose paddled closer until he could clamber out of the water and hide amongst the crowd of waterfowl. A hand reached out and he stepped back in fear. But hunger got the better of him. The smell of fresh popped corn enticed him closer and he began to eat ravenously and without caution.

The goose was not the only lost soul that was hiding out beside the water. A young teenage boy, who had run from a harsh father, was camped under trees at the far end of the lake. He had been scavenging from the waste bins of the houses in the neighbourhood and also by catching the occasional crawfish. He had seen the old woman coming to this same spot each day with her bag of corn. He had also noted that each time

she left there was one less large plump duck amongst the dwindling group.

The boy had heard the heartbroken goose as he had paddled aimlessly through the water and his own heart had gone out to the large bird. Now he watched from behind an old tree trunk as the old woman cackled and clucked as the corn disappeared into the goose's beak. The young lad was horrified as he could see that this was not going to end well. At risk to his own safety he dashed from behind the tree and pushed the wrinkled crone sideways. She toppled over and slipped off her perch into the water screaming abuse at her assailant.

He scooped up the goose and turned away from the startled ducks that flapped off in panic. He dare not turn around in case the witch put a curse on him and his heavy companion. He skittered out into the narrow road and raced as fast as his legs could carry him. Up ahead he saw a large black gate with a small gap to the side of it. It was very narrow, but he was half-starved, and if he turned sideways he could just squeeze himself and his now struggling burden through.

The goose was indignant and getting into a right strop. He was totally unaware of the danger he had been in. Or the fact, that if he not been hauled unceremoniously from the feast he had been enjoying, he would now be in a witch's kitchen with a roasting hot future ahead of him.

Heaving a massive sigh of relief the boy loosened his grip on the goose slightly and the bird turned its head towards a new sound. The lad lifted his face up to find himself staring into the eyes of an enormous lion. The great beast was bedecked with two butterflies, fluttering their wings in the heat of the midday sun.

'I am a guardian of the secret garden and you have trespassed. What have you to say for yourself boy before I turn you to stone?'

The boy was petrified. He had come from a home where strength had been measured in how many slaps you could administer to a child before they ran away. He closed his eyes and felt sick with fright. He also felt guilty that he had indeed run away, and left his two younger brothers behind to face a similar fate.

The goose wriggled in his arms and the lad looked down at the long graceful neck of this spirited bird. He took a long breath and began hesitantly to tell their story. As the words flowed so did his passion and his determination not to desert another vulnerable creature.

He risked looking deep into the lion's eyes and as he finished his tale, he imagined he saw a softening in the stern gaze and even the butterflies appeared to stop fluttering their wings in anticipation.

After a moment the lion nodded his great maned head and told the boy to sit on a stone bench before him.

'I know of the witch of whom you speak,' he rumbled. 'She was blown here across the seas from a place called Scotland many moons ago. I believe she had purchased a new broom and the test flight was not as uneventful as expected.'

The big cat paused as his recollections came back to him. 'She could not speak the lingo of course and was like a fish out of water over here in Spain. She tried to steal food but the locals around here are handy with their hunting rifles and soon saw her off.'

A long rumbling laugh came from his huge belly. 'She had a craving for something deep-fried that was a delicacy back in her native city and she decided that crispy fried fairies might make up for its lack in her diet.' He paused for affect.

'She came over the hedge one dark night in a stealth attack on the occupants under the magnolia tree when they come out to dance. However one of my eagles who was on patrol spotted the old besom… pardon the pun!'

'He dived down and plucked the evil crone out of the night sky and flew her fifty miles away to the forest… Unfortunately looks like she has found her way back again.'

The boy and the now quietened goose listened enraptured by the story but were shaken out of their reverie as the lion cleared his throat loudly.

"Hmmm… well this does not solve the problem… there are only two choices available to trespassers. Go back the way you came or be turned to stone.' He looked down, not unkindly, at the now quaking pair.

'Perhaps there might be a compromise but I will need to confer with the other guardians and the Fairy Queen first. I will send out my personal assistants to enquire of the others what your fate should be. They have your story and will relate it on their journey.'

He realised that the two must be hot and thirsty having sat for hours in the baking sun. 'Off you go now to the fountain of life and drink. Then sit in the shade until I call for you.' With that he dismissed the pair to a leafy part of the garden.

The boy cupped his hand and filled it with sweet water, offering it to the grateful goose first before drinking his fill. As they quenched their thirst they saw the two butterflies take flight on the journey that would decide their fate. The goose showed no inclination to run from the boy and settled down on his lap as they waited in the shade of the tree.

The butterflies had been given strict instructions about who they needed to contact in the secret garden, but first they stopped off at the eagles station to ensure that air cover would be available in case of a witch attack.

Having established a safe airspace the messengers continued to a private part of the garden where the resident therapist, Dr. Filibuster Buck (who moon-lighted in the Stoned Band as the back-up singer) was in a session with Pearly Girl. Anyone who knew the sweet child understood that therapy was necessary due to her constant frustration levels with her stoned band. The seven dwarves who comprised the garden's orchestra where an emotional bunch.

Wiffy never seemed to be happy, Sniffy was still using the sneezeweed and then there was Ditsy, who was as daft as a brush.

Anyway, the butterflies appeared at an opportune moment in the session and both Doc Buck and Pearly Girl listened with interest and cast their vote.

After leaving Dr. Buck and his patient, the butterflies did a circuit of the garden collecting votes from the various residents, before ending up at the magic magnolia tree. They needed to collect the final votes from the fairy queen, her new toy boy husband and her hundreds of subjects who lived in the roots and undergrowth. It was dusk so they hovered in the leaves until the moon lit the branches and the first fireflies glowed above the pathways and homes beneath them. Before long a court page ushered them into the palace. A place where we humans cannot follow....

In their leafy part of the garden both boy and goose lay asleep in the soft grass… The bird had eaten the tender green shoots and drunk more water and now lay cuddled against the beating heart of the boy. It was the first time since he had lost his beloved mate that he felt safe and he was content.

The boy too had eaten some of the fruit that had hung from the branches above his head, and as he clasped the warm feathered chest against his own, he prayed that they would be allowed to stay together in this sanctuary.

As the moon rose in the sky he heard the flutter of wings above his head and he knew their fate had been decided. He gently cradled the sleepy goose and followed the colourful messengers back to the lion and stood before him quietly.

'The decision has been made,' the lion said gravely. 'The inhabitants of this secret place do not wish to put you at harm from that old witch so have offered you a choice.'

The boy held his breath and the waking goose seemed to understand how important the next words might be for their future.

The lion continued. 'You can leave of your own free will if you wish. However, if you would like to remain here in safety you will be turned to stone and become apprentice guardians under my tutelage. You will help protect the smaller citizens of this world from evil like the witch and the goose will make an excellent and very loud sentry.'

The boy let out a long sigh and looked down at the goose in his arms. The bird was alone too, and as he had mated for life, he would continue to wander the migration route in solitude. The decision was an easy one. He smiled at the lion who nodded in pleasure. The two butterflies flew to each side of the pair and the boy felt himself lifted up high in the air.

Gently the two large flying beasts carried the boy and the goose to a ledge overlooking the mountains, under the shelter of a jutting roof with strong stone to the back and sides of them. As the butterflies released their precious cargo the boy felt a wave of peace begin at his feet and spread up through his body.

The goose turned to stone in his arms and the last human thought that he felt was happiness... they were safe and together they would become the best guardians ever of this magical sanctuary.

~ ~ ~

Chapter 8
The Boy, his Dog and a Fairy Princess

The toddler waddled across the damp grass, falling down from time to time with a resounding thump onto his backside. He giggled and struggled onto all fours until he could stand again. His blonde curly hair shone in the mid-morning sun and his old nurse looked on with pride as her young charge explored his domain.

There had been great joy at the boy's birth. The owners of the house had waited many years and suffered terrible losses but finally, one bright winter's day, the strong and healthy cry of a newborn was heard throughout the magic garden. The fairies beneath the magnolia tree held a celebration that night and as the statues that guarded the garden came to life, music could be heard tinkling through the snow covered branches.

Eighteen months later the boy was beloved by all he came into contact with. His parents would have been astonished to find out that even the magical inhabitants of the garden adored him too. In fact, as he had slept in his carriage in the shade of the magnolia tree, he had been sprinkled with fairy dust to protect him.

Now as the young master played in the grass he was unaware that a young fairy had ventured out into the daylight. Normally the folk who lived beneath the magnolia only came out at night after the humans had gone to bed, but lured by the happy giggling of the infant, an inquisitive fairy had sneaked out of the palace gates.

As she perched on one of the branches, her glittery purple wings drew the eye of the child. He focused on the shimmering vision in the tree and pointed with his little fingers at the young fairy. The two of them stared at each other for a brief moment until the spell was broken by the nurse sweeping the child up into her arms. But that brief moment was profound. A bond was formed that would grow stronger and stronger as the years passed.

With no other children in the family it was decided on the young master's fifth birthday that he should be given a companion in the form of a robust puppy. As he played with the furry ball of love, he glanced upwards to the tree to see if his secret friend was watching. She was not there and even though he was still only a child, he felt sadness that the fairy was not present to share this special day.

Many years passed and the young boy and his dog grew to adulthood. They spent every free minute of the day together when the boy was not in school. They roamed the mountainside around the house and the dog slept at the end of the bed each night. As they played in the garden they were often observed. Cloaked with invisibility, the now teenage fairy princess kept a watchful and loving eye from her perch in the tree.

When the boy was eighteen years old; disaster struck. War was declared and he was conscripted into the local militia to protect the town and farms in the district. His terrified parents watched him march away through the gate in his polished black boots with his heavy knapsack. His old dog now weary with arthritis whined as he lay at their feet.

Days and nights passed and the humans lay in bed listening to the sound of canon fire in the distance. After many months of fighting the enemy forces retreated and the militia followed them to the borders. It had been several desperate months since they had word from their son and they feared the worst. They could also see that the old dog was losing his will to live as he pined away.

It seemed that the magic garden and all the inhabitants were holding their collective breath. Then one spring morning, as the old and short-sighted dog wandered out to his position on the steps where he would lie all day watching the gate; a miracle occurred.

There before him was a pair of dusty black boots and excitedly the dog sniffed around the leather. He smelt his master and with his worn out heart beating like a bass drum, he followed the scent down the steps and around the back of the house.

Curled up in a ball beneath the magnolia tree was the body of a man with long dirty blonde hair and

clothes that were torn and matted with filth. But the dog showed no hesitation as he licked the dirt from his beloved master's face. The man stirred and reached out a hand to stroke the grey-tipped ears and tears streaked his mud covered face.

All night the man had been watched over by another creature whose own tears had fallen upon his body as he slept. The fairy princess had sat by his head as he tossed and turned in his troubled dreams, gently stroking his hair and whispering loving words to him. As he had calmed, she had gently snipped a lock of his long blonde hair and plaited it into a bracelet. She may never be able to love him in human ways but she would always wear this to keep him close.

The excited barking of the dog alerted the family and servants and they rushed out to the garden to find the reason for the uproar… As the delighted family embraced and then carried the young man into the house, the princess returned to the palace in the roots of the magnolia, where she found her stone-faced mother waiting for her in the throne room.

A few weeks later, when the returned soldier was fully recovered and peace had been declared, his parents decided to hold a ball for all their neighbours to celebrate. This was the first fiesta for many years and everyone dusted off their finery and the musicians from the town tuned up neglected instruments. The garden was festooned with garlands and tables were covered with a magnificent array of foods.

The handsome young host, now fully recovered greeted the guests but still glanced from time to time at the magnolia tree, wondering if perhaps he might catch a glimpse of his beautiful fairy. He began to move away to talk to his guests but a flash of turquoise caught his eye. As he turned his head a shimmering image appeared before him out of thin air and he caught his breath.

There, sat in a bower made of roses, was the most enchanting woman he had ever seen.

She smiled and held out her hand to him. Around her delicate wrist he noticed a woven bracelet of blonde hair and gold that glistened in the sunlight. The instant they touched an electric charge raced from his fingertips to his heart and he knew who this beautiful stranger was.

'How long can you stay?' he asked in a desperate whisper.

'Forever, my love,' she smiled gently. 'My mother has gifted me one hundred years to share with you. But only if that is what you desire?'

They lived happily ever after and as a reward for his long and loyal service the old dog became a guardian of the magic garden. And at night when his beloved master and his wife strolled hand in hand across the lawns, their friend would walk beside them, young and playful again.

~ ~ ~

Chapter 9

The Last Summer Ball
and the Winter Fairy

I t was a lovely end of summer afternoon and all within the magic garden was quiet. It was siesta time and most of the inhabitants, both in the fairy kingdom beneath the magnolia tree, and the stone guardians were napping. They needed their rest, as

tonight was the last ball of the season, and for days everyone had been racing around in preparation.

There had been an early start to this summer with very high temperatures in early May. The heat had continued to suck the moisture out of the air for the last few months. For the humans this meant extra work watering the foliage which brought colour and wildlife to the magic garden. But now the temperatures had settled down to provide warm but gentle days, which were welcomed by all who shared this special place.

The head of the guardians was worn out. The fairy queen was being particularly demanding about the preparations for the dance tonight and he now dozed in the late afternoon warmth.

'Psst, psst,' came a persistent buzz in the large guardian's ear. He decided to ignore what was surely an uneducated insect who clearly did not who he was pssting.

'Psst, master, psst,' clearly a very, very ignorant insect.

The lion opened one eye and glanced to his right. He groaned inwardly and resigned himself to some wasted time of nonsense.

Eager to impart some nugget of news to the head guardian, Fizzy the rabbit looked up adoringly at the lion.

'He's been seen, he's coming, we have to do something, he is on his way, we have to panic.'

The lion looked down at Fizzy and shook his head slowly from side to side. Of all the creatures under his care this was the one who caused the most problems. Since a young rabbit, he had been a sugar addict; craving what was commonly called the Amber Nectar. If you wanted to find Fizzy you just had to head towards the nearest Amber joint and he would have his whiskers deep in the blooms.

It was clear that Fizzy had made a stop off at the nearest amber bar and was going to be hyper for the next hour. The lion knew he would get no peace until he had listened to the whole story and just hoped he had enough time to finish his nap before the ball.

'Slow down Fizzy and tell me what the problem is,' the guardian said patiently to the rabbit who was bouncing up and down on his tail.

'The Winter Fairy is on his way and is bringing a very, very cold front with him,' the rabbit drew breath. 'He will reach us tonight during the ball and everyone in the garden will be frozen in place and visible to the humans forever.'

'Okay Fizzy just who saw him and where?' The lion was slightly more concerned now this was potentially catastrophic.

'My Irish cousins were playing near their burrow a few days ago and heard him cursing and ranting in the trees above their heads.' Fizzy held out one of his paws to the lion and touched his leg.

'They sent a pigeon to bring me the message and it says he is bored stupid with hanging around for October and wants to get on with his job now.'

This was not good news. The lion knew that he had to warn the Fairy Queen and the other inhabitants of the garden. The most immediate decision concerned tonight's festivities. At night all the statues came to life for a few precious hours. If they and the fairies were unexpectedly frozen in place and visible to humans, the magic garden would cease to exist.

He had to think and he couldn't do that with the excited rabbit bouncing up in down in fear. He gently sent Fizzy on his way and called in his butterflies who acted as his messengers within the garden. Their first priority was to find the Fairy Queen and call the counsellors together for a cabinet meeting.

The last the lion had heard, his queen was indulging in some retail therapy in preparation of tonight's ball. A tad disrespectfully for this venerable guardian, he did wonder what she needed with another pair of shoes and a new hat.

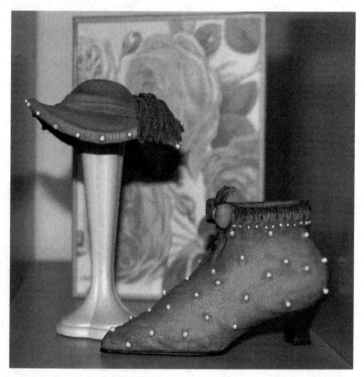

To be fair, the Fairy Queen was thinking just that herself when the delicate butterfly alighted on the back of her chair with a vital message from her head guardian. With a wistful last look at the jewelled shoes and matching hat, she turned and headed back to the palace beneath the magnolia tree accompanied by the messenger.

The queen called together her ministers and they all listened as the guardian spoke remotely through his intermediary. Clearly this was a dangerous situation. Not just because they would have to cancel the ball,

but because the preparations for the winter were not complete. Without the usual stores of honey stored in nutshells in the cellars of the palace, there would not be enough food for the fairy population during the longer than usual dark months.

Just then another butterfly flew into the chamber and delivered even more devastating news. Reports had arrived in from the French Fairy Federation or the FFF's; that the Winter Fairy had put a spurt on and was only a few hours away.

The Fairy Queen, Filigree, called her counsellors together to put into action the Disaster Prevention Plan they had hoped never to activate.

Before making her final decisions about the operation, the queen called upon the toothless gnome who was the fairy soothsayer. Spread out on the table in front of her, placed on the magic blue silk cloth, was the gnome's crystal ball.

Her majesty was getting impatient and snapped at the quivering figure standing before her. 'Well, what are you waiting for? she glared at the poor creature. 'Are we definitely going to be in for an early freeze?

The gnome had rarely been called upon during his five hundred years in his capacity of soothsayer, and

was not sure if his magic divining powers were still working. He waved his hands over the crystal ball and muttered the magic words loudly for maximum dramatic effect.

'Bumble, grumble, fumble, crumble'.

Queen Filigree and her courtiers leaned in and gasped in horror. The crystal ball had clouded into ice crystals before their very eyes. None were more surprised than the gnome who hid a delighted and relieved toothless grin behind his gnarly hands.

'Right,' said the queen having composed herself. She pointed at one of her closest advisors.

'Ampletum, I want you to go immediately and take a message to the Queen Bee,' She closed her eyes for a moment as she gathered her thoughts.

'Tell her majesty that this devastating cold front is coming in within hours and her hives are in danger. Suggest that she have a final sweep of the last of the summer roses with her swarm and then retreat down into our honey cellars. This will provide us with much needed stores for the winter and a safe place for them to stay warm.'

Ampletum hurried off to do his queen's bidding; trembling nervously at the important task he had been assigned.

The queen looked around her chamber and her eyes fell upon one of the cheekiest of her fairy advisors. Pinchit was a bit of a rogue but he knew everything that was happening in the garden at any given time and this task would require his specialist knowledge.

She beckoned him over and whispered in his tufted ear. 'Find me Fluffy,' she looked at his wily little face. 'I know you know where that rascal is and I need

you to go to whatever rock or log he is hiding under and bring him to me immediately.'

Pinchit bowed his head and scurried off to climb up the staircase through the magnolia roots to the magic garden. He headed off around the corner of the villa to the uncultivated wasteland by the back fence. It was a safe bet that he would find the sun loving Fluffy basking himself on the hot sand.

Pinchit spent a few minutes explaining the dire situation they were all facing. Fluffy, first and foremost was concerned about himself. Dragons do not like the cold which is why they have their own internal combustion system. He thanked Pinchit for the warning and was about to turn away to find some safe place in the foundations of the villa when the fairy tapped him on his nose.

'The Queen is demanding that you come with me Fluffy as she has a special job for you.' Pinchit hooked one of his fingers through the dragon's nostril and muttered menacingly. 'She said not to take no for an answer.'

Ten minutes later Fluffy settled down on his haunches and glared at the Fairy Queen. In her long reign these two had been at loggerheads as her royalness was unimpressed by the dragon's habit of starting little fires in the garden when he sneezed. This happened a lot in the spring when the pollen count was high, and despite the fairies giving him a very potent anti-histamine, he refused to take prescribed medica-tion of any kind.

Queen Filigree came down off her high horse, commonly called her throne, and sat in front of Fluffy. She held out her hands and smiled at the bemused dragon. 'I would like you to do me a great favour,' she paused and prayed she would choose the right words for this vital request.'

Meanwhile just an hour away to the north tiny snow-flakes began to fall on the parched earth. It settled quickly as the inhabitants looked out of their homes in amazement. Animals and insects alike were caught unawares and already the fatal cold claimed its first victims.

Out in the magic garden the Queen Bee had rallied her swarm and accepted the invitation issued by the Fairy Queen. Bees visited every last summer rose in the garden and made their way, heavily laden through the roots of the magnolia tree into the honey caverns beneath. Here special honey fairies directed the thousands of insects into the roof of the specially constructed cellars, where they began to build an intricate honeycomb.

The fairy kingdom would now have sufficient supplies for the long winter ahead and the bees could reside in safety away from the devastating cold.

As these preparations continued the Fairy Queen knew that she had to do something to raise the spirits of those beneath the magnolia and also amongst her stone guardians in the magic garden. Wrapping herself in a cloak of gold silk that kept the chill from her delicate bones, she visited each member of her loyal entourage.

The Stoned Dwarf band huddled beneath the old oak tree in the fading sunlight and looked at her sadly. They had been rehearsing for the last three months to perform in tonight's final ball of the summer and now this would not take place. She gently touched them on their pointed heads and requested that they strike up a song to keep the rest of the garden in

high spirits as they went about their urgent tasks. Before long the cheerful sound of music reached every corner of the magic kingdom.

The queen also flew down to the sandy wasteland at the back of the garden and perched for a few minutes on a small mound of rocks. Beneath her, with chest expanded to its fullest extent, Fluffy blew hot breath northwards. With the help of a snuff box of fairy dust, the dragon was able to extend his normal range by fifty miles. He was tiring but he had managed to keep

the freezing cold front at bay for that very important extra few hours.

His reward was to spend the winter months in a specially prepared fire-proof chamber in the royal palace. The queen happily reflected that the extra heating would be very welcome once they got into the deepest and darkest nights of winter!

Finally the preparations were complete. The Fairy Queen had visited all her statues within the garden and with the final trail of insects and one very tired but satisfied dragon, she retreated to the warmth and safety beneath the magnolia tree.

As a special surprise and a thank you to all her subjects and the special guests, her Majesty had opened up the giant ballroom and had the firefly chandeliers dusted off. Instead of the Dwarf Stoned band, in the corner of the ornate chamber, an old fashioned gramophone was wound up and the air was filled with the sounds of a Viennese Waltz. The delighted fairies and their guests took to the floor as the fireflies created an aerial display that took their breath away.

With Fluffy safely tucked up for the winter and without his magic dragon breath, the cold front advanced rapidly. The Winter Fairy flew into the magic garden delighted with his childish prank. He stood in the deep snow and looked around him excitedly. Instead of frozen fairies, insects and out of place statues there was... nothing. Just one obnoxious fairy, alone and barely visible in a blanket of white.

~ ~ ~

Chapter 10
Mollie (The Duchess) Coleman

My daughter thought that I might like to introduce some of my many gardens to you as a break from her own and my other daughter's beautiful surroundings. I am afraid that I have to go back nearly 90 years to describe my first real garden but luckily I do have one or two photographs to share with you. It is a tough ask to cram 94 years into 1000 words which is what my daughter expects, so I do hope you bear with me!

I never knew my father. For a few months after I was born in the October of 1917, he and my mother Georgina lived in Kent where he was undergoing re-training. He had been badly wounded whilst rescuing his officer and had been awarded the Military Medal. He had been told that he would not be returning to the front and that his role would now only be administrative. They decided to start a family and my Irish father named me Mollie Eileen Walsh.

He was 31 years old when he was killed on November 2nd 1918, just nine days before peace was declared. As people rejoiced in the streets of Britain my mother waited for news. It was to be three weeks after the war before she was finally informed that he was not coming home. She did not know where he was buried and sadly she and I had to move on with our lives without him.

My mother's family were from Alverstoke in Hampshire and also Bramdean in the rural part of the county. She decided we should move closer to her home and so we arrived in the lovely village of Wickham, famous for its square and horse fairs. We lived in a small cottage off the square but I don't really remember much of those early years.

When I was seven my mother remarried the village butcher, Norman Welch and he built us a new home on Hoad's Hill which led into the village from Fareham and Portsmouth. As well as the modern house we had a

wonderfully large garden with a small orchard of fruit trees. The following 15 years were a wonderful mixture of village hall dances and bright summer days. Here I am in our orchard at the back of the house which was called *Sinclair*.

Then another war shattered our hopes of peace and life in the village changed overnight. However, in late 1939, a friend of mine in the Royal Navy introduced me to a tall and handsome electrical artificer named Eric Coleman and within a very short time we knew that we wanted to get married. We made plans to have the wedding on Saturday September 14th 1940, but on the Monday, Eric was given orders to join a convoy leaving for Canada on Thursday 12th and was confined to barracks.

To cut a very long story short.... our vicar got on the telephone to Eric's commanding officer and persuaded him to allow him leave to marry me on the 11th, returning in time for the ship the next day. The whole village pulled together to get my dress finished and the grocery shop, that shut on Wednesday afternoons, opened to get a cake and sandwiches together for our guests. The vicar's wife arrived in her car to drive me to the church where I found my handsome husband-to-be.

We had to return to *Sinclair* for the impromptu reception and the German bombers decided that they would add their contribution by dropping bombs on Portsmouth. Since they would often jettison any left on the countryside on their return flight we did some ducking and diving ourselves.

Here is our wedding party after the all clear including my giant red cat who looked more like a fox. Ironically because of the bombing the night before, Eric's transport ship left early and he missed it. As I moped around in the garden after just one night of honeymoon, and not expecting to see him for at least a year, he walked in the front door with a week's leave!

Wedding day. Wednesday September 11th 1940

I travelled all over England to be with Eric any time he had shore leave throughout the next two years. In 1942 we had our first daughter Sonia and we moved to Scotland to Dunoon to join Eric who was based there repairing submarines. Our second daughter Diana was born there in 1943. Eric then returned to sea and did not return from the Far East and Ceylon (Sri Lanka) until late in 1946.

Sonia and Diana. Sinclair 1944

We had settled back into the house on Hoad's Hill but sadly my mother who had ill health died in 1945 aged only 52. My step-father moved into a cottage in Fareham and as a family we enjoyed being in our own home and garden for the first time since the beginning of the war. Our third daughter Sally was born in 1953 and Eric was posted to Sri Lanka in 1955. As it was for a two year posting we all went with him. Now that was a garden... or should I say jungle!

We had snakes and monkeys outside the front door and often inside. It was not unusual to find small monkeys helping themselves to my lipstick and pearl earrings on my dresser having let themselves in the window. And we were not just treated to exotic wildlife in our garden. The navy is very good at providing a wonderful social life but travelling back at night could be interesting with leopards and elephants on the move on the narrow road through the jungle.

However, we had an incredible time and arrived back to our home in Wickham in time for our son Jeremy to be born in 1957.

We moved to Old Portsmouth in 1958 to a modern house with a very strange garden... the house was built on the site of an old public house that existed before the Battle of Trafalgar. It had been bombed during the war and three new houses were built as a terrace on the site. However the small garden was built over the old wine cellar of the pub which now served as our garage. Without trees and a lawn I had to make use of old wooden wine caskets that I picked up locally and turned into planters. Every summer I would fill them with pink geraniums and each winter with pansies.

In 1959 we were posted to Malta and then in 1963 to 1965 we lived in South Africa. This was followed by two years in Lancashire before returning in 1967 to Portsmouth for good. When Eric retired we moved across the high street into a lovely flat but my garden became even smaller.

However, we did have a flat roof and I placed all my planters up the wrought iron stairs and around the roof top. Here I am completing the small crossword in The Daily Telegraph with my coffee which is something I enjoyed doing each morning.

We had many wonderful years in the flat, and rather than travel overseas, we made short trips to Scotland, Wales, Jersey and other beautiful parts of Britain. One of the many things that had attracted me to Eric in the first place was that he was a wonderful dancer. We loved nothing better than going away to stay in hotels

that had dinner dances on the Saturday nights and we were still dancing all through our 70s.

We would also visit public gardens and would sit in the shade on benches and enjoy their beauty.

Sadly after 56 years together Eric passed away and a year later at age 80 I moved across the road again to my little house with its small front and back gardens. Here I was to live for the next 14 years and my greatest pleasure was keeping my small piece of heaven stocked with geraniums and pansies. My living room window was large and offered me a wonderful view of

all the visitors to the garden including foxes, hedgehogs and blackbirds in search of raisins.

There are some gardens that hold very special memories for me. Diana had done some research and early in the 90s had managed to establish where my father was buried. He was in a small military cemetery in a village called Poix-du-Nord along with about twenty of his fallen comrades. I visited with Diana and her husband and then again with Sally who was living in Brussels, only 65 kilometres from his final resting place. It was very emotional to finally see my father's

name carved in granite and I hope that he would have been proud to know that he left behind a family of many bright and happy grandchildren and great-grandchildren.

Diana and her husband lived around the corner from me and I would often take advantage of her larger garden. I would sit quietly for hours watching her dog chasing squirrels and the many different species of birds popping into visit.

The years passed and before I knew it I was 94 years old… What a journey and how lucky I had been to

have seen so much of the world and enjoyed so many gardens in the company of someone who loved me so much. And if you are wondering? I would be hard pushed to tell you what my favourite flower is but I can tell you without a shadow of a doubt that if it is pink, it is beautiful.

Oh and if you are wondering too about *The Duchess* nickname, it is probably because I was rather partial to buying and wearing beautiful jackets, and I was rarely seen without my pearls! I rather insisted on being dressed and ready for the day by 9.00 each morning even if there was nothing on the calendar... I firmly believe that you should be prepared to meet people looking your best. I suspect some might have thought I was a bit grand....

Anyway it was no longer possible for me to remain in my house but I will always remember that last view through the window and the sight of my little fairy princess in the alcove. It is engraved on my heart.

From where I sit now I can watch my daughter's little black Staffie chasing squirrels and also seeing off the postman and anyone else who dares intrude on this sanctuary. If you catch sight of me perhaps you could do me a great favour and pop a large, cut-glass tumbler of whisky and water, no ice thank you, on the table beside me. I am finding it rather difficult to get hold of these days.

All the best…
and don't forget that whisky and water will you!

Mollie Eileen Coleman
October 5th 1917 to July 28th 2012
The Duchess

The End

About the Book

We look out into our gardens and spend time keeping the hedges immaculate and the lawns trimmed. Flower beds and rose bushes provide the colour that tempts us to sit in deck chairs as we inhale the scent of the blossoms.

But, eyes may be watching and secret treasures may lie undisturbed beneath that old tree in the corner. Have you ever wondered why that garden gnome is out of place or there is a gleam of glitter amongst the leaves of the hedge?

Tales from the Garden reveals those secrets and more. Stone statues and hidden worlds within the earth are about to share their stories. The guardians who have kept the sanctuary safe for over fifty years will allow you to peek behind the scenes of this magical place. They will take you on a journey through time and expand your horizons as they transport you to the land of fairies, butterflies and lost souls who have found a home here.

Next time you pass that moss laden statue at the end of your garden; stop and touch with your hand. Can you feel that? That heartbeat.

Fairy Stories for children of all ages from five to ninety-five that will change the way you look at your garden forever.

About the Author

Sally Cronin spent a number of years in each of the following industries – Retail, Advertising and Telecommunications, Radio & Television; and has taken a great deal of inspiration from each.

She has written short stories and poetry since a very young age and contributed to media in the UK and Spain. In 1996 Sally began studying nutrition to inspire her to lose 150 lbs and her first book, Size Matters published in 2001, told the story of that journey back to health. This was followed by another seven books across a number of genres including health, humour and romance.

For the last two years Sally has written a daily blog covering the subjects close to her heart and it is called *Smorgasbord Invitation – Variety is the Spice of Life.* You can link to it from here:

smorgasbordinvitation.wordpress.com

Sally Cronin

Also by Sally Georgina Cronin

Size Matters… Especially if you weigh 330 lbs!
moyhill.com/sm
Print: ISBN 97819055997024
MOBI: ISBN 9781905597475
EPub: ISBN 9781905597468

Just Food For Health
Print: ISBN 9781905597239

Forget the Viagra… Pass Me a Carrot!
moyhill.com/ftvpmac
Print: ISBN 9781905597420
MOBI: ISBN 9781905597437
EPub: ISBN 9781905597277

Turning Back the Clock
moyhill.com/tbtc
MOBI: ISBN 9781905597574
EPub: ISBN 9781905597581

Media Training The manual
moyhill.com/mttm
Print: ISBN 9781905597314
MOBI: ISBN 9781905597567
EPub: ISBN 9781905597321

Sam, A Shaggy Dog Story
moyhill.com/sam
Print: ISBN 9781905597413
MOBI: ISBN 9781905597451
EPub: ISBN 9781905597352

Just an Odd Job Girl
moyhill.com/jaojg
Print: ISBN 9781905597123
MOBI: ISBN 9781905597550
EPub: ISBN 9781905597543

Flights of Fancy
moyhill.com/fof
MOBI: ISBN 9781905597598
EPub: ISBN 9781905597604

E-books available through Moyhill.com Amazon and Smashwords.

Size Matters

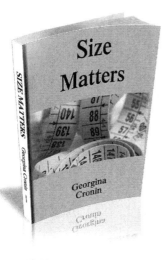

I wanted to find answers to explain how I had managed to eat and starve myself to 330 lbs. This book is my story, but it is also the blueprint of the program that you will be following.

Print: ISBN 97819055997024
MOBI: ISBN 9781905597475
EPub: ISBN 9781905597468
moyhill.com/sm

If any of these feels familiar… then this book is definitely for you!

- You can't take a bath because you can't get out again
- You don't even fit sideways into the shower
- You get desperate late at night when the chocolate shops are shut
- You are ashamed to take your clothes off in front of yourself
- You don't fit into airline seats and have to have a seat belt extension
- You struggle to get out of the car
- You can barely walk 10 minutes down the road
- You can't fit into public toilets
- People ask you when the baby is due
- You hate shop assistants coming into the too-small changing rooms
- You have stopped doing everything you once loved to do
- You have stopped sharing activities with the ones you love
- You are obsessed with where your next food is coming from
- You crave sweet foods
- You wish it would all go away

Forget the Viagra ... Pass Me a Carrot!

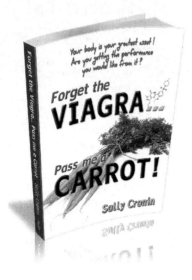

Print: 9781905597420
MOBI: 9781905597437
EPub: 9781905597277
<u>moyhill.com/ftvpmac</u>

Don't die of Ignorance!

If you have ever taken Viagra, or are thinking of taking it, then you need to read this book!

One of the biggest dangers is that many of the men who feel the need to use Viagra are also in the same group who should NOT take the drug because of pre-existing medical conditions. If all you do is read the Health Warning at the front of this book you will be more aware of the dangers you may be exposed to, including heart attack or, worse, death.

We seem to have entered the era of the 'quick fix'. Even the NHS is suggesting that we are unable to change our lifestyles to improve our health and are suggesting a blanket prescription of Statins to over 50s to prevent the future burden of heart disease and dementia. A medication that has side effects including a reduction in hormone levels and in some cases impotence!

This book is aimed at all men who want to be healthy and active into old age – and their partners who are interested in keeping them fit and well.

It is about understanding the amazingly complex ways that our bodies work and keep us alive.

If you understand what your body needs, and respect its organs and systems by taking action and giving them the right fuel (nutrition), you are well on the way to living a longer and healthier life. Without the need for pills for life or a 'quick fix' for your libido.

****

Changing your lifestyle and diet is not a 'quick fix' but once accomplished it will last a lifetime.

Contents include ...

Part One:

A guide to the body and its essential organs and the lifestyle diseases that contribute to male impotence.

Including The Brain, Male Productive System, Hormone production, Obesity, The Blood, Circulatory System, Heart disease, The Liver, Cholesterol, Diabetes, Candida Albicans, Acidity, and Stress.

Part Two:

The Essential nutrients, vitamins and minerals we need to fuel our bodies with.

Part Three:

The essential foods to include in out diet to provide these nutrients, shopping list, eating plan and recipes. Followed by an exercise programme from couch potato to fit and healthy.

Just Food For Health

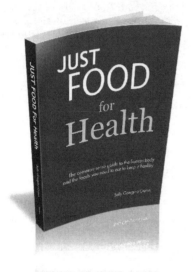

Print: ISBN 9781905597239

A new guide to a healthy lifestyle

'*Just food for Health*' is a comprehensive and common-sense guide to the body and the foods we need to eat to keep it healthy. Intended for the whole family, it covers not only how the body and major organs such as the heart and lungs, liver and kidneys function but what foods are necessary to keep them healthy at all ages.

The modern diet is filled with processed foods, high in sugars and unnatural fats. It is no wonder that, despite amazing advances in medical science, we still have far too many diseases that are lifestyle related.

The book also covers seasonal illnesses, dangers in our food such as additives, how to detox safely and healing foods and herbs.

Whether you want to lose weight safely and permanently or would like to make healthy changes to your diet and lifestyle, '*Just food for Health*' informs you how.

Sam, A Shaggy Dog Story

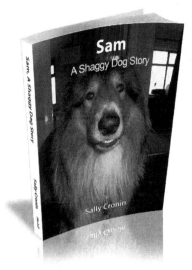

Print: ISBN 9781905597413
MOBI: ISBN 9781905597451
EPub: ISBN 9781905597352
moyhill.com/sam

The Story of Sam and his friends

Millions of families around the World believe that their pet, dog or cat is most intelligent, beautiful and loyal friend that anyone could have. And they are absolutely right.

From the first moment that I met Sam, when he was just three weeks old, his personality and charm shone from his button eyes. Like many pet owners, we were convinced he understood every word we spoke and he actually could say one or two himself. Rather than tell his story from our perspective I have given him a voice and let him tell his own.

I can only imagine what he really thought about his two and four-legged friends but I do hope he loved us as much as we adored him and the time he spent with us shining brightly in our lives.

If only our pets could talk how much richer the world would be and funnier.

Turning Back the Clock

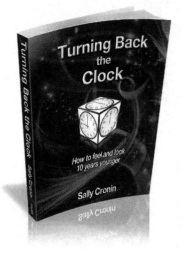

MOBI: ISBN 9781905597574
EPub: ISBN 9781905597581
moyhill.com/tbtc

Living forever is not an option.

The maximum lifespan a human being can currently expect is around 120 years. Making healthy diet and lifestyle choices as early as possible will help your body and mind get as near as possible to that age whilst enjoying good physical and mental vitality.

Turning Back the Clock is a guide to how we can make sensible decisions about our health and diet whilst enjoying a continued quality of life. Not many of us really want to be 90 or 100 years old if it means that we are going to be filled with medication and tucked away in a nursing home unaware of our surroundings.

Every organ in our body requires optimum nutrition, oxygen and exercise to ensure it is running smoothly. As we age our nutritional requirements change and a review from time to time will identify simple adjustments to ensure that health and vitality is maintained.

In the book you will find not just nutritional guidance – including the foods that help anti-aging – but will also help you understand how our attitudes and external appearance can add years to our actual age.

Whilst we all might want to gain that extra ten years at the end of our lives it is actually easier to turn the clock back now and regain the last ten instead. Turning Back the Clock may help you achieve that.

Media Training: The Manual

Print: ISBN 9781905597314
MOBI: ISBN 9781905597567
EPub: ISBN 9781905597321
moyhill.com/mttm

A quick reference manual for anyone who needs the deliver their message via "the Media", TV, Radio, Print.

It is rumoured that the art of communication has been lost but actually it has simply been adapted and expanded to suit the new technologies. However, we still use our voices and radio and television are very powerful tools that can enable us to reach hundreds or even thousands of people in the space of a few minutes.

Those few minutes can have an enormous impact. By reaching out and engaging with an audience you can increase sales, sell your latest book, raise more funds for your charity or inform the public about an event or important community issue.

This guide to media training is about opening the door to that opportunity and making the most of the experience.

Just an Odd Job Girl

Print: ISBN 9781905597123
MOBI: ISBN 9781905597550
EPub: ISBN 9781905597543
moyhill.com/jaojg

Imogen was fifty!

She had been married to Peter for over twenty years and having brought up her children she was living in a wonderful house, with money and time to spare.

Suddenly, she finds herself 'traded-in' for a younger model, a 'Fast-Tracker'. Completely devastated, she retreats to a small house on the edge of Epping Forest, where she indulges in binge eating and self-deprecation. Finally, when she can no longer fit into her clothes, and there seems to be no hope, she discovers a way forward.

Helped by a new friend, she rediscovers herself, making a journey to her past that enables her to move on to her future.

Flights of Fancy

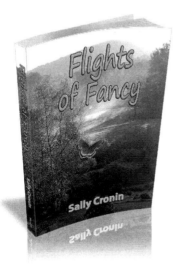

MOBI: ISBN 9781905597598
EPub: ISBN 9781905597604
moyhill.com/fof

Heaven, ghosts as well as romance, revenge and a little murderous intent …

As a child I was fascinated by fairy tales and ghost stories. Ghosts never frightened me and I always thought that they were simply messengers from another world. I have sensed rather than seen spirits myself, but I know that there are places that I have visited that seemed beautiful to look at but felt very cold and unwelcoming, as if there was a darker presence inhabiting the house. I have also found at times that something or someone has pulled me back from taking an action that might well have been harmful to me. Some believe in guardian angels and others that we have an ingrained sixth sense or survival instinct that protects us. All I know is that I am prepared to be open to the possibilities.

In this collection of my short stories, and a novella, you will find my perception of heaven, ghosts as well as romance, revenge and a little murderous intent. I have also given a voice to some of the animals that I have had the privilege to meet in my life to date and I believe that if they could speak for themselves this world would be a better place!